# SUPERHEROES

## DON'T CLEAN UP THEIR ROOMS ...OR DO THEY?

## A Story about the Power of Organization

Written by Zack Bush and Laurie Friedman

Illustrated by Sarah Van Evera

Dedicated to you,
our wonderful reader—
a **SUPERHERO** in training.

Ace and Ava loved **SUPERHEROES**.
They wanted to be **SUPERHEROES**.

They wanted to do things **SUPERHEROES** did.

Battle bad guys.

Save cities.

Protect the planet.

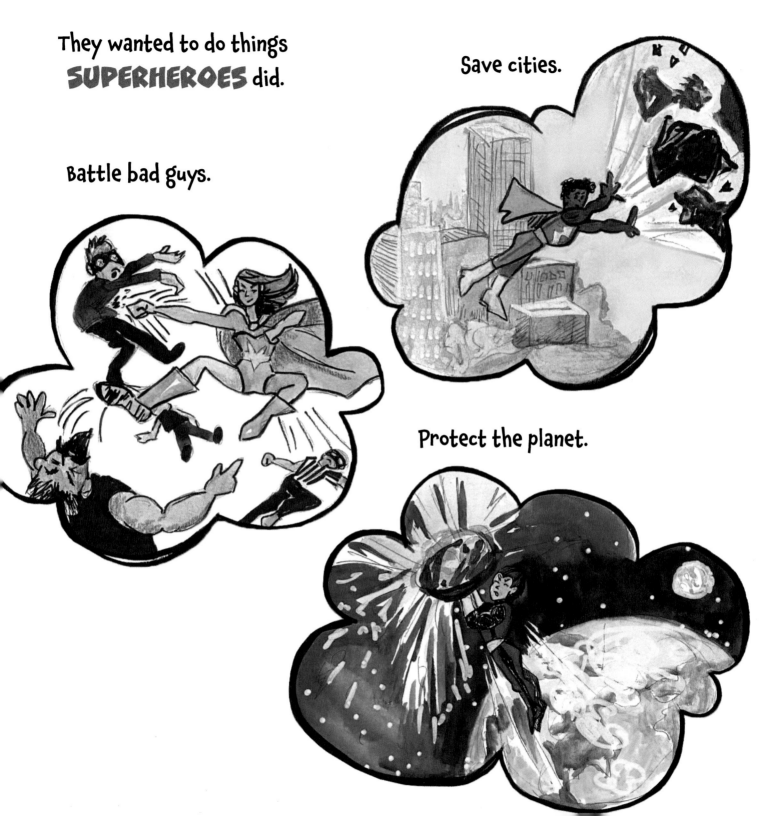

"If we're going to be **SUPERHEROES**, we have to act like **SUPERHEROES**," said Ava.

"First, we'll learn to jump over tall buildings, like real **SUPERHEROES,**" explained Ace. He stacked their blocks high so he and Ava could practice jumping.

Ace and Ava
started to jump.
They jumped.
And they jumped.
And they jumped.

But jumping over tall buildings wasn't as easy as they thought.

"Real **SUPERHEROES** have super strong muscles," said Ava. "Let's try lifting heavy things."

Ace and Ava tried to
lift the chair. They tried.
And they tried.
And they tried.
When they finally did,
everything fell
on the floor.

He and Ava looked for their
**SUPERHERO** sneakers.
The ones that made
them run **super** fast.

They couldn't find them, but they started to run anyway. They ran, and they ran, slipping and sliding through the house, UNTIL . . .

"We're being **SUPERHEROES**," Ace said.
"yeah, **real SUPERHEROES**," added Ava.

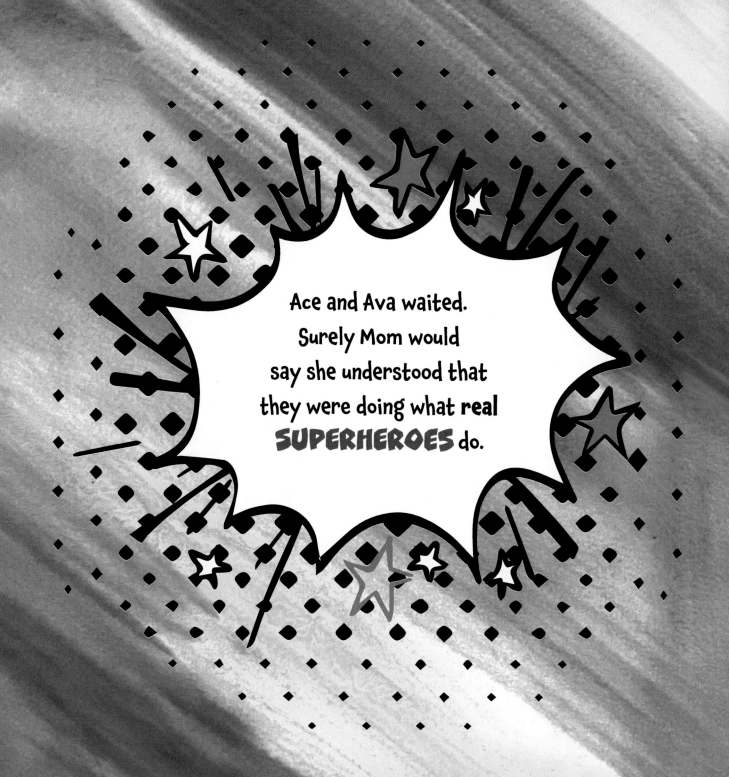

Ace and Ava waited.
Surely Mom would
say she understood that
they were doing what **real**
**SUPERHEROES** do.

But Mom said, "You **CANNOT** run through the house!" Then she marched Ace and Ava up the stairs.

"YOU NEED TO CLEAN UP THIS ROOM!"
said Mom when she saw the mess they had made.

"But **SUPERHEROES** don't clean up their rooms," said Ace.
"yeah," said Ava. "**Real SUPERHEROES** don't clean up their rooms."

Ace's shoulders slumped. "We're never going to be real **SUPERHEROES**."

Ava shook her head sadly. "Never!"

Ace and Ava climbed down from the bed and started to clean their room.
They put board game pieces back into the right boxes.
They lined up their books.

They made sure all of the stuff they
had knocked over went back where it belonged.

Ace and Ava put blocks into the bin marked BLOCKS and toys into the chest marked TOYS.

"Cleaning up isn't so bad," said Ace.

"Organizing is kind of fun," said Ava.

Ace and Ava straightened the stuffed animals on their shelves.

They picked up clothes off the floor.

They tucked in the sheets and blankets on their beds.

"Wow!" said Ava when they finished.
"We have so much more room to be **SUPERHEROES**!"

Ace even found their
**SUPERHERO** sneakers.

When Mom saw how well everything was organized, she gave Ace and Ava a big hug and said, "Real **SUPERHEROES** are great at cleaning their rooms!"

She even gave them a **SUPERHERO** badge to prove it.

Follow these simple
steps, and you can earn your
**SUPERHERO ORGANIZATION BADGE** too:

Step 1:  Organize your toys.
Step 2:  Put things away.
Step 3:  Straighten your shelves.
Step 4:  Pick up your clothes.
Step 5:  Make your bed.